THE
DELEGATE
from Venus

THE DELEGATE
from Venus

Henry Slesar

ÆGYPAN PRESS

This story from *Amazing Science Fiction Stories,* October, 1958.

Henry Slesar often published his story under the pseudonym
E.K. Jarvis.

Special thanks to Greg Weeks, Stephen Blundell and the
Online Distributed Proofreading Team (which can be found
at http://www.pgdp.net).

The Delegate from Venus
A publication of
ÆGYPAN PRESS

www.aegypan.com

Everybody was waiting to see what the delegate from Venus looked like. And all they got for their patience was the biggest surprise since David clobbered Goliath.

"*L*et me put it this way," Conners said paternally. "We expect a certain amount of decorum from our Washington news correspondents, and that's all I'm asking for."

Jerry Bridges, sitting in the chair opposite his employer's desk, chewed on his knuckles and said nothing. One part of his mind wanted him to play it cagey, to behave the way the newspaper wanted him to behave, to protect the cozy Washington assignment he had waited four years to get. But another part of him, a rebel part, wanted him to stay on the trail of the story he felt sure was about to break.

"I didn't mean to make trouble, Mr. Conners," he said casually. "It just seemed strange, all these exchanges of couriers in the past two days. I couldn't help thinking something was up."

"Even if that's true, we'll hear about it through the usual channels," Conners frowned. "But getting a senator's secretary drunk to obtain information — well, that's not only indiscreet, Bridges. It's downright dirty."

Jerry grinned. "I didn't take *that* kind of advantage, Mr. Conners. Not that she wasn't a toothsome little dish . . ."

"Just thank your lucky stars that it didn't go any further. And from now on —" He waggled a finger at him. "Watch your step."

Jerry got up and ambled to the door. But he turned before leaving and said:

"By the way. What do *you* think is going on?"

"I haven't the faintest idea."

"Don't kid me, Mr. Conners. Think it's war?"

"That'll be all, Bridges."

*T*he reporter closed the door behind him, and then strolled out of the building into the sunlight.

He met Ruskin, the fat little AP correspondent, in front of the Pan-American Building on Constitution Avenue. Ruskin was holding the newspaper that contained the gossip-column item which had started the whole affair, and he seemed more interested in the romantic rather than political implications. As he walked beside him, he said:

"So what really happened, pal? That Greta babe really let down her hair?"

"Where's your decorum?" Jerry growled.

Ruskin giggled. "Boy, she's quite a dame, all right. I think they ought to get the Secret Service to guard her. She really fills out a size 10, don't she?"

"Ruskin," Jerry said, "you have a low mind. For a week, this town has been acting like the *39 Steps,* and all you can think about is dames. What's the matter with you? Where will you be when the big mushroom cloud comes?"

"With Greta, I hope," Ruskin sighed. "What a way to get radioactive."

They split off a few blocks later, and Jerry walked until he came to the Red Tape Bar & Grill, a favorite hangout of the local journalists. There were three other newsmen at the bar, and they gave him snickering greetings. He took a small table in the rear and ate his meal in sullen silence.

It wasn't the newsmen's jibes that bothered him; it was the certainty that something of major importance was happening in the capitol. There had been hourly conferences at the White House, flying visits by State Department officials, mysterious conferences involving members of the Science Commission. So far, the byword had been secrecy. They knew that Senator Spocker, chairman of the Congressional Science Committee, had been involved in every meeting, but Senator Spocker was unavailable. His secretary, however, was a little more obliging . . .

Jerry looked up from his coffee and blinked when he saw who was coming through the door of the Bar & Grill. So did every other patron, but for different reasons. Greta Johnson had that effect upon men. Even the confining effect of a mannishly-tailored suit didn't hide her outrageously feminine qualities.

She walked straight to his table, and he stood up.

"They told me you might be here," she said, breathing hard. "I just wanted to thank you for last night."

"Look, Greta —"

Wham! Her hand, small and delicate, felt like a slab of lead when it slammed into his cheek. She left a bruise five fingers wide, and then turned and stalked out.

*H*e ran after her, the restaurant proprietor shouting about the unpaid bill. It took a rapid dog-trot to reach her side.

"Greta, listen!" he panted. "You don't understand about last night. It wasn't the way that lousy columnist said —"

She stopped in her tracks.

"I wouldn't have minded so much if you'd gotten me drunk. But to *use* me, just to get a story —"

"But I'm a *reporter,* damn it. It's my job. I'd do it again if I thought you knew anything."

She was pouting now. "Well, how do you suppose I feel, knowing you're only interested in me because of the Senator? Anyway, I'll probably lose my job, and then you won't have *any* use for me."

"Good-bye, Greta," Jerry said sadly.

"What?"

"Good-bye. I suppose you won't want to see me any more."

"Did I say that?"

"It just won't be any use. We'll always have this thing between us."

She looked at him for a moment, and then touched his bruised cheek with a tender, motherly gesture.

"Your poor face," she murmured, and then sighed. "Oh, well. I guess there's no use fighting it. Maybe if I *did* tell you what I know, we could act *human* again."

"Greta!"

"But if you print one *word* of it, Jerry Bridges, I'll never speak to you again!"

"Honey," Jerry said, taking her arm, "you can trust me like a brother."

"That's *not* the idea," Greta said stiffly.

In a secluded booth at the rear of a restaurant unfre-quented by newsmen, Greta leaned forward and said:

"At first, they thought it was another sputnik."

"*Who* did?"

"The State Department, silly. They got reports from the observatories about another sputnik being launched by the Russians. Only the Russians denied it. Then there were joint meetings, and nobody could figure out *what* the damn thing was."

"Wait a minute," Jerry said dizzily. "You mean to tell me there's another of those metal moons up there?"

"But it's not a moon. That's the big point. It's a spaceship."

"A *what?*"

"A spaceship," Greta said coolly, sipping lemonade. "They have been in contact with it now for about three days, and they're thinking of calling a plenary session of the UN just to figure out what to do about it. The only hitch is, Russia doesn't want to wait that long, and is asking for a hurry-up summit meeting to make a decision."

"A decision about what?"

"About the Venusians, of course."

"Greta," Jerry said mildly, "I think you're still a little woozy from last night."

"Don't be silly. The spaceship's from Venus; they've already established that. And the people on it — I *guess* they're people — want to know if they can land their delegate."

"Their what?"

"Their delegate. They came here for some kind of conference, I guess. They know about the UN and everything, and they want to take part. They say that with all the satellites being launched, that our affairs are *their* affairs, too. It's kind of confusing, but that's what they say."

"You mean these Venusians speak English?"

"And Russian. And French. And German. And everything I guess. They've been having radio talks with practically every country for the past three days. Like I say, they want to establish diplomatic relations or something. The Senator thinks that if we don't agree, they might do something drastic, like blow us all up. It's kind of scary." She shivered delicately.

"You're taking it mighty calm," he said ironically.

"Well, how else can I take it? I'm not even supposed to *know* about it, except that the Senator is so careless about —" She put her fingers to her lips. "Oh, dear, now you'll really think I'm terrible."

"Terrible? I think you're wonderful!"

"And you promise not to print it?"

"Didn't I say I wouldn't?"

"Y-e-s. But you know, you're a liar sometimes, Jerry. I've noticed that about you."

*T*he press secretary's secretary, a massive woman with gray hair and impervious to charm, guarded the portals of his office with all the indomitable will of the U. S. Marines. But Jerry Bridges tried.

"You don't understand, Lana," he said. "I don't want to *see* Mr. Howells. I just want you to *give* him something."

"My name's not Lana, and I *can't* deliver any messages."

"But this is something he *wants* to see." He handed her an envelope, stamped URGENT. "Do it for me, Hedy. And I'll buy you the flashiest pair of diamond earrings in Washington."

"Well," the woman said, thawing slightly. "I *could* deliver it with his next batch of mail."

"When will that be?"

"In an hour. He's in a terribly important meeting right now."

"You've got some mail right there. Earrings and a bracelet to match."

She looked at him with exasperation, and then gathered up a stack of memorandums and letters, his own envelope atop it. She came out of the press secretary's office two minutes later with Howells himself, and Howells said: "You there, Bridges. Come in here."

"Yes, *sir!*" Jerry said, breezing by the waiting reporters with a grin of triumph.

There were six men in the room, three in military uniform. Howells poked the envelope towards Jerry, and snapped:

"This note of yours. Just what do you think it means?"

"You know better than I do, Mr. Howells. I'm just doing my job; I think the public has a right to know about this spaceship that's flying around —"

*H*is words brought an exclamation from the others. Howells sighed, and said:

"Mr. Bridges, you don't make it easy for us. It's our opinion that secrecy is essential, that leakage of the story might cause panic. Since you're the only unauthorized person who knows of it, we have two choices. One of them is to lock you up."

Jerry swallowed hard.

"The other is perhaps more practical," Howells said. "You'll be taken into our confidence, and allowed to accompany those officials who will be admitted to the landing site. But you will *not* be allowed to relay the story to the press until such a time as *all* correspondents are informed. That won't give you a 'scoop' if that's what you call it, but you'll be an eyewitness. That should be worth something."

"It's worth a lot," Jerry said eagerly. "Thanks, Mr. Howells."

"Don't thank me, I'm not doing you any *personal* favor. Now about the landing tonight —"

"You mean the spaceship's coming down?"

"Yes. A special foreign ministers conference was held this morning, and a decision was reached to accept the delegate. Landing instructions are being given at Los Alamos, and the ship will presumably land around midnight tonight. There will be a jet leaving Washington Airport at nine, and you'll be on it. Meanwhile, consider yourself in custody."

*T*he USAF jet transport wasn't the only secrecy-shrouded aircraft that took off that evening from Washington Airport. But Jerry Bridges, sitting in the rear seat flanked by two Sphinx-like Secret Service men, knew that he was the only passenger with non-official status aboard.

It was only a few minutes past ten when they arrived at the air base at Los Alamos. The desert sky was cloudy and starless, and powerful searchlights probed the thick cumulus. There were sleek, purring black autos waiting to rush the air passengers to some unnamed destination. They drove for twenty minutes across a flat ribbon of desert road, until Jerry sighted what appeared to be a circle of newly-erected lights in the middle of nowhere. On the perimeter, official vehicles were parked in orderly rows, and four USAF trailer trucks were in evidence, their radarscopes turning slowly. There was activity everywhere, but it was well-ordered and unhurried. They had done a good job of keeping the excitement contained.

He was allowed to leave the car and stroll unescorted. He tried to talk to some of the scurrying officials, but to no avail. Finally, he contented himself by sitting on the sand, his back against the grill of a staff car, smoking one cigarette after another.

As the minutes ticked off, the activity became more frenetic around him. Then the pace slowed, and he knew the appointed moment was approaching. Stillness returned to the desert, and tension was a tangible substance in the night air.

The radarscopes spun slowly.

The searchlights converged in an intricate pattern.

Then the clouds seemed to part!

"Here she comes!" a voice shouted. And in a moment, the calm was shattered. At first, he saw nothing. A faint roar was started in the heavens, and it became a growl that increased in volume until even the shouting voices could no longer be heard. Then the crisscrossing lights struck metal, glancing off the gleaming body of a descending object. Larger and larger the object grew, until it assumed the definable shape of a squat silver funnel, falling in a perfect straight line towards the center of the light-ringed area. When it hit, a dust cloud obscured it from sight.

A loudspeaker blared out an unintelligible order, but its message was clear. No one moved from their position.

Finally, a three-man team, asbestos-clad, lead-shielded, stepped out from the ring of spectators. They carried geiger counters on long poles before them.

Jerry held his breath as they approached the object; only when they were yards away did he appreciate its size. It wasn't large; not more than fifteen feet in total circumference.

One of the three men waved a gloved hand.

"It's okay," a voice breathed behind him. "No radiation . . ."

Slowly, the ring of spectators closed tighter. They were twenty yards from the ship when the voice spoke to them.

"Greetings from Venus," it said, and then repeated the phrase in six languages. "The ship you see is a Venusian Class 7 interplanetary rocket, built for one-passenger. It is clear of all radiation, and is perfectly safe to approach. There is a hatch which may be opened by an automatic lever in the side. Please open this hatch and remove the passenger."

An Air Force General whom Jerry couldn't identify stepped forward. He circled the ship warily, and then said something to the others. They came closer, and he touched a small lever on the silvery surface of the funnel.

A door slid open.

"It's a box!" someone said.

"A crate —"

"Colligan! Moore! Schaffer! Lend a hand here —"

A trio came forward and hoisted the crate out of the ship. Then the voice spoke again; Jerry deduced that it must have been activated by the decreased load of the ship.

"Please open the crate. You will find our delegate within. We trust you will treat him with the courtesy of an official emissary."

They set to work on the crate, its gray plastic material giving in readily to the application of their tools. But when it was opened, they stood aside in amazement and consternation.

There were a variety of metal pieces packed within, protected by a filmy packing material.

"Wait a minute," the general said. "Here's a book —"

He picked up a gray-bound volume, and opened its cover.

"'Instructions for assembling Delegate,'" he read aloud. "'First, remove all parts and arrange them in the following order. A-1, central nervous system housing. A-2 . . .'" He looked up. "It's an instruction book," he whispered. "We're supposed to *build* the damn thing."

*T*he Delegate, a handsomely constructed robot almost eight feet tall, was pieced together some three hours later, by a team of scientists and engineers who seemed to find the Venusian instructions as elementary as a blueprint in an Erector set. But simple as the job was, they were obviously impressed by the mechanism they had assembled. It stood impassive until they obeyed the final instruction. "Press Button K . . ."

They found button K, and pressed it.

The robot bowed.

"Thank you, gentlemen," it said, in sweet, unmetallic accents. "Now if you will please escort me to the meeting place . . ."

*I*t wasn't until three days after the landing that Jerry Bridges saw the Delegate again. Along with a dozen assorted government officials, Army officers, and scientists, he was quartered in a quonset hut in Fort Dix,

New Jersey. Then, after seventy-two frustrating hours, he was escorted by Marine guard into New York City. No one told him his destination, and it wasn't until he saw the bright strips of light across the face of the United Nations building that he knew where the meeting was to be held.

But his greatest surprise was yet to come. The vast auditorium which housed the general assembly was filled to its capacity, but there were new faces behind the plaques which designated the member nations. He couldn't believe his eyes at first, but as the meeting got under way, he knew that it was true. The highest echelons of the world's governments were represented, even — Jerry gulped at the realization — Nikita Khrushchev himself. It was a summit meeting such as he had never dreamed possible, a summit meeting without benefit of long foreign minister's debate. And the cause of it all, a placid, highly-polished metal robot, was seated blithely at a desk which bore the designation:

VENUS

The robot delegate stood up.

"Gentlemen," it said into the microphone, and the great men at the council tables strained to hear the translator's version through their headphones, "Gentlemen, I thank you for your prompt attention. I come as a Delegate from a great neighbor planet, in the interests of peace and progress for all the solar system. I come in the belief that peace is the responsibility of individuals, of nations, and now of worlds, and that each is dependent upon the other. I speak to you now through the electronic instrumentation which has been created for me, and I come to offer your planet not merely a threat, a promise, or an easy solution — but a challenge."

The council room stirred.

"Your earth satellites have been viewed with interest by the astronomers of our world, and we foresee the day when contact between our planets will be commonplace. As for ourselves, we have hitherto had little desire to explore beyond our realm, being far too occupied with internal matters. But our isolation cannot last in the face of your progress, so we believe that we must take part in your affairs.

"Here, then, is our challenge. Continue your struggle of ideas, compete with each other for the minds of men, fight your bloodless battles, if you know no other means to attain progress. But do all this *without* unleashing the terrible forces of power now at your command. Once unleashed, these forces may or may not destroy all that you have gained. But we, the scientists of Venus, promise you this — that on the very day your conflict deteriorates into heedless violence, we will not stand by and let the ugly contagion spread. On that day, we of Venus will act swiftly, mercilessly, and relentlessly — to destroy your world completely."

Again, the meeting room exploded in a babble of languages.

"The vessel which brought me here came as a messenger of peace. But envision it, men of Earth, as a messenger of war. Unstoppable, inexorable, it may return, bearing a different Delegate from Venus — a Delegate of Death, who speaks not in words, but in the explosion of atoms. Think of thousands of such Delegates, fired from a vantage point far beyond the reach of your retaliation. This is the promise and the challenge that will hang in your night sky from this moment forward. Look at the planet Venus, men of Earth, and see a Goddess of Vengeance, poised to wreak its wrath upon those who betray the peace."

The Delegate sat down.

*F*our days later, a mysterious explosion rocked the quiet sands of Los Alamos, and the Venus spacecraft was no more. Two hours after that, the robot delegate, its message delivered, its mission fulfilled, requested to be locked inside a bombproof chamber. When the door was opened, the Delegate was an exploded ruin.

The news flashed with lightning speed over the world, and Jerry Bridges' eyewitness accounts of the incredible event was syndicated throughout the nation. But his sudden celebrity left him vaguely unsatisfied.

He tried to explain his feeling to Greta on his first night back in Washington. They were in his apartment, and it was the first time Greta had consented to pay him the visit.

"Well, what's *bothering* you?" Greta pouted. "You've had the biggest story of the year under your byline. I should think you'd be tickled pink."

"It's not that," Jerry said moodily. "But ever since I heard the Delegate speak, something's been nagging me."

"But don't you think he's done good? Don't you think they'll be impressed by what he said?"

"I'm not worried about that. I think that damn robot did more for peace than anything that's ever come along in this cockeyed world. But still . . ."

Greta snuggled up to him on the sofa. "You worry too much. Don't you ever think of anything else? You should learn to relax. It can be fun."

She started to prove it to him, and Jerry responded the way a normal, healthy male usually does. But in the middle of an embrace, he cried out:

"Wait a minute!"

"What's the matter?"

"I just thought of something! Now where the hell did I put my old notebooks?"

He got up from the sofa and went scurrying to a closet. From a debris of cardboard boxes, he found a worn old leather brief case, and cackled with delight when he found the yellowed notebooks inside.

"What *are* they?" Greta said.

"My old school notebooks. Greta, you'll have to excuse me. But there's something I've got to do, right away!"

"That's all right with me," Greta said haughtily. "I know when I'm not wanted."

She took her hat and coat from the hall closet, gave him one last chance to change his mind, and then left.

Five minutes later, Jerry Bridges was calling the airlines.

*I*t had been eleven years since Jerry had walked across the campus of Clifton University, heading for the ivy-choked main building. It was remarkable how little had changed, but the students seemed incredibly young. He was winded by the time he asked the pretty girl at the desk where Professor Martin Coltz could be located.

"Professor Coltz?" She stuck a pencil to her mouth. "Well, I guess he'd be in the Holland Laboratory about now."

"Holland Laboratory? What's that?"

"Oh, I guess that was after your time, wasn't it?"

Jerry felt decrepit, but managed to say: "It must be something new since I was here. Where is this place?"

He followed her directions, and located a fresh-painted building three hundred yards from the men's dorm. He met a student at the door, who told him that Professor Coltz would be found in the physics department.

The room was empty when Jerry entered, except for the single stooped figure vigorously erasing a blackboard. He turned when the door opened. If the students looked younger, Professor Coltz was far older than Jerry remembered. He was a tall man, with an unruly confusion of straight gray hair. He blinked when Jerry said:

"Hello, Professor. Do you remember me? Jerry Bridges?"

"Of course! I thought of you only yesterday, when I saw your name in the papers —"

They sat at facing student desks, and chatted about old times. But Jerry was impatient to get to the point of his visit, and he blurted out:

"Professor Coltz, something's been bothering me. It bothered me from the moment I heard the Delegate speak. I didn't know what it was until last night, when I dug out my old college notebooks. Thank God I kept them."

Coltz's eyes were suddenly hooded.

"What do you mean, Jerry?"

"There was something about the Robot's speech that sounded familiar — I could have sworn I'd heard some of the words before. I couldn't prove anything until I checked my old notes, and here's what I found."

He dug into his coat pocket and produced a sheet of paper. He unfolded it and read aloud.

"'It's my belief that peace is the responsibility of individuals, of nations, and someday, even of worlds . . .' Sound familiar, Professor?"

Coltz shifted uncomfortably. "I don't recall every silly thing I said, Jerry."

"But it's an interesting coincidence, isn't it, Professor? These very words were spoken by the Delegate from Venus."

"A coincidence —"

"Is it? But I also remember your interest in robotics. I'll never forget that mechanical homing pigeon you constructed. And you've probably learned much more these past eleven years."

"What are you driving at, Jerry?"

"Just this, Professor. I had a little daydream, recently, and I want you to hear it. I dreamed about a group of teachers, scientists, and engineers, a group who were suddenly struck by an exciting, incredible idea. A group that worked in the quiet and secrecy of a University on a fantastic scheme to force the idea of peace into the minds of the world's big shots. Does my dream interest you, Professor?"

"Go on."

"Well, I dreamt that this group would secretly launch an earth satellite of their own, and arrange for the nose cone to come down safely at a certain time and place. They would install a marvelous electronic robot within the cone, ready to be assembled. They would beam a radio message to earth from the cone, seemingly as if it originated from their 'spaceship.' Then, when the Robot was assembled, they would speak through it to demand peace for all mankind . . ."

"Jerry, if you do this —"

"You don't have to say it, Professor, I know what you're thinking. I'm a reporter, and my business is to tell the world everything I know. But if I did it, there might not be a world for me to write about, would there? No, thanks, Professor. As far as I'm concerned, what I told you was nothing more than a daydream."

*J*erry braked the convertible to a halt, and put his arm around Greta's shoulder. She looked up at the star-filled night, and sighed romantically.

Jerry pointed. "That one."

Greta shivered closer to him.

"And to think what that terrible planet can do to us!"

"Oh, I dunno. Venus is also the Goddess of Love."

He swung his other arm around her, and Venus winked approvingly.

THE END